MW00886979

Where Is My Voice?

Tracey Lawrence

SRL Publishing

www.srlpublishing.co.uk

#BreakingTheSilence

SRL Publishing Ltd
42 Braziers Quay
Bishop's Stortford
Herts, CM23 3YW

First published worldwide by SRL Publishing in 2017
Second edition in 2018

Copyright © Tracey Lawrence and Sean Webster

The author and illustrator reserves the right to be identified as the author of this work.

ISBN: 978-0995732322

All rights reserved. No part of this publication may be reproduced or transmitted in any form or by any means, electronic, mechanical, photocopying or otherwise, without the prior permission of the publishers.

For Amy and the Lawrence's who continue to support me to be able to write and to all of the children that continue to inspire me daily.

"Hello. My name is Poppy."

Poppy is a happy girl. She loves her family, friends and loves nothing more than playing with her toys and running around in her garden.

She loves singing along to music and playing teacher at home with her teddies.

At school she had friends, loved reading stories and enjoyed difficult Maths questions. But there was one thing that Poppy found difficult...

talking.

Ever since Poppy could remember, she hadn't spoken to anybody except her Mum, Dad and little brother Toby. She COULD talk, but she just couldn't speak in public places.

In the playground, she ran around with the other children. She knew what to say but she couldn't find her voice.

In a restaurant she knew what she wanted to eat. Poppy wanted to ask the waitress but she couldn't find her voice.

In the shop she wanted to say 'thank you', but she couldn't find her voice.

One night when the sun had gone down and the stars were twinkling in the sky, Poppy sat on her bed and cried.

Her Mum appeared at the door, saw that Poppy was crying and gave her a HUGE cuddle. "Where is my voice, Mum?"
"It's deep inside you, Poppy. We just need to find the key to unlock it." "I know" replied Poppy. "I find it so hard. It just feels like a huge lump in my throat and I panic."

The very next day Poppy's Mum took her to the doctors. Her Mum explained all about how hard Poppy found it to speak in public places and that they didn't know how to help her.

Dr Perry sat there nodding and smiling over at Poppy who smiled back nervously.

Dr Perry asked Poppy, "Can you talk?" She nodded furiously. "Ah then I know just the person that can help". Dr Perry told Poppy's Mum all about her friend called Jenny who had worked with other children who had had the same problem before.

'Other children?' Poppy thought to herself.

Dr Perry waved off Poppy and her Mum as Poppy bounded towards the car with a skip in her step.

As she jumped in and turned on the radio she said to her Mum, "So there are other children who are the same as me?". Her Mum smiled and nodded as they made their way home.

Later as Poppy sat down for her dinner she excitedly told her Dad and little brother Toby all about Dr Perry, Jenny and their conversation.

That night, Poppy crawled into bed. "Mum, do you think Jenny will be able to help me? Do you really think that I can do this?" "Poppy I have complete faith in you. You're such a strong girl.

Poppy was awoken by the sound of birds tweeting and sunlight creeping in through her curtains. She got herself dressed, played with Toby and ate her breakfast. Poppy felt butterflies in her tummy. Her Mum gave her a reassuring smile. Then she set off with Mum to go to Jenny's house.

As they pulled onto the driveway they were greeted by a friendly woman. She had long brown hair and eyes that twinkled. Poppy felt her tummy settle a little more. Jenny looked like one of her teachers at school.

As they went inside, Poppy looked around. She saw pictures on the walls of lots of other children. They all had smiley faces. In the photo's she saw another familiar face that she recognised – Jenny!

Hmmmm, they must be Jenny's children, she thought to herself. At this point Jenny saw Poppy looking at the picture and must have known what she was thinking as she explained, "I bet you're wondering who those children are? They are the children that I have worked with in the past. They are all very special to me, as are you." Poppy felt herself smile and blush.

Jenny + Flo

Poppy saw some toys in the living room, sat down on the floor and   started playing with them. Jenny sat beside her. She explained a little more about the children that she had worked with before. "I knew another little girl just like you. She had the most beautiful voice but there were times that she couldn't find it"

Poppy listened. Jenny continued, "We worked together and set some goals."

"I bet that you do try to find your voice, don't you?" Jenny said. Poppy nodded. "But maybe you feel a little worried at times?", Jenny continued. Poppy kept nodding, her smile turning into a sad face. "I have an idea!" Jenny rushed into the kitchen. Poppy looked at her Mum who gave her another reassuring smile.

When Jenny returned, Poppy noticed that she had a little yellow pouch in her hand. It was a drawstring bag.

Poppy wondered what was inside. As Jenny opened the bag she exclaimed, "Worry dolls!"

"These are little worry dolls. You keep them under your pillow at night. When you have a worry, take one out and   whisper your worry to the doll. Then pop it back into the bag, pull the string and put the bag back under your pillow. Whilst your sleeping, the worry dolls will take your worries away".

Jenny handed the dolls to Poppy. These are a present from me to you. Poppy flashed a huge grin and gave Jenny the biggest cuddle.

"Let's set our first goal. Poppy, I want you to think tonight of someone that you will talk to. Your first goal". And with that Poppy smiled at Jenny, took her worry dolls and went home with her Mum.

That night Poppy took out her worry dolls
and whispered some of her worries to them.

She smiled, tucked them under her pillow and
drifted off to sleep whilst thinking of the
person that she wanted to speak to the most.

The following week Poppy packed her worry dolls and skipped off to Jenny's with a   letter in the pocket in her dress. As she skipped in the door Jenny questioned, "Have you been using the worry dolls?" Poppy smiled and nodded happily then handed her letter to Jenny.

She opened it to see the name, Emily. Jenny knew that it was their first goal. Emily was Poppy's best friend. They played together at school.   Poppy had always wanted to invite Emily to come for tea. Her Mum had already arranged play dates in the past and Poppy had loved it but SHE wanted to be the one to ask Emily. Jenny nodded in approval.

Jenny and Poppy went blackberry picking and decided to make a crumble. As they were baking, Jenny sneezed. Flour went everywhere and she burst out laughing. Poppy let out thc tiniest giggle then froze. With a hand on Poppy's shoulder Jenny winked. "Now that was MY first goal". She continued, "Now Poppy, let's have the smallest target. I want you to say hi to Emily on Monday at school. I know that this will be huge for you". Poppy's eyes said it all.

The panic on her face was evident. Jenny saw this and followed it up with, "That worry that you're feeling – share it with your worry dolls. And when you feel those feelings that you're feeling now – breathe...deeply. Count down from 5 and speak on 1 – practise at home".

Later on that day Poppy was colouring in. She remembered Jenny had told her to practise. "5.. 4.. 3.. 2.. 1.. – Hi" It didn't feel hard to say but she knew that it wouldn't be easy.

On Monday morning although she felt that lump in her throat and the butterflies in her stomach, Poppy felt determined. "I'm going to do it!" she said to Toby who was playing with his porridge at the dinner table. He responded with babbles.

Emily ran up to Poppy on the playground as she usually did. "Hi Poppy!" Emily called.

Poppy felt like she was frozen, the hairs stood up on the back of her neck and she felt like running.

5..

4..

3..

2..

1..

She whispered, "Hi"

Emily looked gobsmacked as if she'd seen a ghost. Only when she realised it was Poppy, she beamed and they ran off playing together.

When the clock struck 3.30 p.m. Poppy ran out of school and jumped into her Mum's car. "I found my voice! I found my voice!"

She retold the story of the day's events to her Mum who was equally as excited. Her Mum gave her a huge cuddle, planted a kiss on her forehead proud of her achievements. "Just you wait until I tell Jenny!" Poppy said proudly.

That week, Poppy burst through Jenny's front door and ran into the garden where she found Jenny planting some potatoes. She thrust a letter into her hand. Neatening out the paper Jenny read it. *I spoke to Emily*!!!!!!

At that moment Poppy threw her arms around Jenny, a tear tumbling down her cheek and whispered ever so slightly,

"Thank you!"

Jenny and Poppy continued to work together week after week, month after month. They set their goals together increasing the number of people that Poppy could speak to.

Teachers, other children, waiters, postmen were all on the receiving end of Poppy's found voice. As her confidence grew, the lump in her throat shrunk, the butterflies in her tummy begun to fly away and her voice began to get louder.

A year later it was an open day at school. Poppy's Mum and Dad couldn't make it as they were both working and Toby was at nursery so Poppy asked Jenny.

"I'd be delighted to come!" she replied.

The day came. Jenny arrived a little earlier but the kind lady at the office said that she could wait outside the classroom. As Jenny sat waiting for the right time, she heard a familiar voice. She stood up and looked through the window. There as proud as a lion was Poppy.

In her hand was a framed photograph of her and Jenny, smiling. Jenny beamed as that was not the only thing. Poppy was proudly telling the whole class the story of her and Jenny. She had finally found her voice.

SRL Publishing and Tracey Lawrence have been delighted to work alongside Selective Mutism charity, *The Voice of My Child*, in producing *Where Is My Voice*.

"Tracey Lawrence, specialist Leader in Education for Behavior and winner of the 2016 Peoples Book Awards, now brings us a new lovely story in a beautifully illustrated book called Where Is My Voice, to help young children who live with Selective Mutism and to raise awareness about this condition.

As having struggled with Selective mutism myself, I find this book to be a great start to let your child know that he is not alone, that there are other children who feel this fear and that it is possible to overcome using simple techniques and support from the right persons."

More info can be found at www.thevoiceofmychild.com

ABOUT THE ILLUSTRATOR

Sean Webster is a children's book illustrator from Liverpool. He has had a passion for drawing from an early age, and gets the bulk of his inspiration from books, films, and famous artists such as Walt Disney and Dr Seuss. *Where Is My Voice* is Sean's first mainstream illustrating contract.

Find him on Twitter here: @seanwebsters

For all of my family. Thank you for being so supportive xx

ABOUT THE AUTHOR

Tracey Lawrence is an Assistant Head teacher at a primary school in Leicestershire. She is also a Specialist Leader in Education for Behaviour. She works with children and adults who display Social, Emotional and Mental Health needs (SEMH) and Special Education Needs and Disabilities (SEND).

Find her on Twitter here: @behaviourteach

Where Is My Voice, is the second in our #BreakingTheSilence series, aimed at helping young children who are going through a difficult time to find their voice, and supporting the parents to enable their children to keep the conversation going at home and at school.

MORE FROM THE PUBLISHER

SRL Publishing is a book publishers based in the UK. Other titles under SRL Publishing include:

Stories of a Supermarket - By Stuart Debar (E-Book only)
The Soul of Destruction - By Marcus Coulson
The Day Poppa Turned Into A Star—By Tracey Lawrence

COMING SOON!

The Black Dog—The next in our #BreakingTheSilence series focussing on depression in children.

The 7.54 - A crime/mystery thriller surrounding a train journey and the murders of its passengers.

Avenged - After finding out their parents past, Michelle and Lee are determined to avenge their death. But will it lead to more tragedy?

CPSIA information can be obtained
at www.ICGtesting.com
Printed in the USA
LVHW072358230321
682295LV00029B/1449